FLY
HOMER
FLY

FLY HOMER FLY

BILL PEET

Houghton Mifflin Company Boston

To my grandson
Timothy

HOMER was a simple farm pigeon who lived in an abandoned barn far out on a grassy hilltop. The ramshackle old barn had lost part of its roof and one wall had tumbled. Still there was plenty of shelter there for the pigeon. In cold weather Homer could always roost in a cozy corner up on a rafter, and during the heat of the summer all the cracks and knotholes let in the cooling breezes.

Homer never had to worry about going hungry. The surrounding fields swarmed with insects of all flavors, so the pecking was always good. He spent the days lazily wandering about the fields snapping up a sowbug here and there, or a beetle, or a caterpillar, or whatever suited his taste.

In the wintertime after all the insects had disappeared it was only a short flight across the field to a chicken yard where he could always count on a feast of cracked corn.

Life for the farm pigeon was simple and easy with never a thing to worry about. However, there were times when he felt lonely all by himself way out there in the country, so lonely it was almost unbearable. Just the same Homer planned to live there for the rest of his days, and he would have, too, if a storm hadn't come rumbling over the countryside one morning.

It wasn't the booming thunder and lightning, or the fiercely howling wind that changed things for Homer. It was a tiny sparrow who came sailing out of the stormy sky. The fierce wind tossed him about like a leaf and the driving rain sent him careening downward. Just when it seemed that the sparrow would be dashed to to the ground one desperate flurry of his wings carried him upward and across a field, then finally on into the old barn, and into Homer pigeon's life.

"It's not much of a day for flying," Homer said to the be-
draggled sparrow who was roosting on a rafter.

"Right you are pidg," said the sparrow, furiously fluttering
his wings to fluff dry himself. "Would you believe I was perched
on a power line in Mammoth City less than an hour ago when
Whoosh! this wham-zammer of a storm grabs on to me and here
I am way out in the middle of nowhere? By the way, pidg, where'd
you blow in from?"

"I live here," said Homer.

"You mean you're a hayseed? A country bumpkin? And you
live here in this pile of old planks?"

"Where should I live?" asked the pigeon.

"Mammoth City. That's where, bumpkin. Pigeon Plaza to be exact. It's a fabulous place. All trees, fountains, statues, and green lawns. And would you believe that people come there just to feed the pigeons? Every day's a feast day at Pigeon Plaza."

"Sounds dandy," said Homer.

"Can't wait to get back," chirped the sparrow, hopping along the rafter for a peek at the sky. "Well whatta ya know!" he exclaimed. "The storm's gone ka-poot! Just like that, clouds and all. So I guess I'll be scootin' along. Meanwhile, bumpkin, give a thought to Pigeon Plaza."

"I have," said Homer, "and I'm ready to go."

"Great! great! great!" cried the sparrow. "So we're off! Ka-zoom!" and he was out of the barn like a shot. In seconds he was sailing a hundred feet in the air, and to his surprise the pigeon was just a wingbeat behind.

"Say now, bumpkin!" he called out, "you're a pretty fair country flyer!"

"My name's Homer," said the pigeon.

"They call me Sparky," said the sparrow, "and now before we go skit-skattin' off in the wrong direction I've got to figure out the whichway of things." Then he began circling around with his bright beady eyes scanning the landscape below.

"Here we go," he said at last. "If I'm right that's Highway Ninety-nine down there. It'll take us straight East, right smack into Mammoth City."

As they went winging along above the highway Homer was surprised at how much traffic there was and how fast it was going. It was one steady stream of autos, trucks, and busses rushing over the hills at a furious pace, each one crowding to get past the other as if there wasn't a second to lose.

"See what I mean?" shouted the sparrow. "Everyone's in a big fat hurry to get to Mammoth City."

"Me too!" cried the pigeon eagerly. He was getting more excited by the mile. Those lonely days out in the country were now a thing of the past. On ahead there was a whole wonderful new life filled with excitement. He could even feel the excitement in the air. At least there was something in the air.

They were flying into a greenish-brown haze that brought tears to the pigeon's eyes.

"My eyes burn," Homer complained.

"That's natural," said Sparky. "This hazy stuff is called smog, which means we're almost there. Just look!"

On ahead of them a great sea of traffic went pouring into tunnels, over bridges past a jumble of factory buildings, and, in the hazy distance beyond, giant skyscrapers rose up through a dense curtain of smog. It was a startling sight to the farm pigeon. He couldn't believe that a place could be so big, or so dark and dreary in the daytime.

"From here on in the flying gets tricky," warned the sparrow. "There's an awful mess of power lines and telephone wires. If you ever hit one, Zango! you're a goner. So stay right on my tail and when I zig you zig, when I zag you zag. OK?"

"OK," said Homer.

In seconds they were into the city sailing along a noisy street jammed with traffic, through a tangle of power lines as thick as cobwebs. And indeed the flying was tricky. Much too tricky for the farm pigeon who was used to fluttering about in the open fields.

Time after time his wing tips brushed the power lines, and he barely managed to dodge a street sign sticking out from a building. It was impossible to keep pace with the darting zigzagging sparrow, and Homer was greatly relieved when at last they came to an open space and Sparky was shouting, "Here we are Homer! Last Stop! Pigeon Plaza!"

And sure enough, directly below them were the green lawns, the trees, the fountains, and the statues, and all the people feeding the pigeons. Great flocks of pigeons.

"It's just like you said!" cried Homer happily. "Even better. It's a wonderful place!"

"The greatest," chirped Sparky, "and like I said, every day's a feast day! Come on, Homer. Let's dive in!"

In the flick of an eyelash the sparrow swooped down into the park and was lost in a milling mob of pigeons crowding around a man who was feeding them bread crusts. It was one big pigeon free-for-all with everyone rudely pushing and shoving. To add to the confusion tiny sparrows went darting in and out of the mob fighting for the crumbs. One of them was Sparky.

"There's more fighting than feasting," thought Homer as he fluttered down to land on the lawn, "and I'm not quite hungry enough to fight for my dinner. Or quite big enough," he added with a sigh. The Plaza pigeons were all much bigger than Homer, and for all he could see they were much tougher too.

As he stood there watching the free-for-all, the man spotted the lone pigeon and tossed him a slice of bread. It was raisin bread, and Homer was delighted.

He had never tasted raisin bread, so this was a special treat.
Seizing it in his beak, he dragged the bread off to a patch of shade
where he could enjoy it in peace.

Just as he was about to take the first peck, suddenly a dozen pigeons came charging at him. They made a wild grab for the bread, and the next thing Homer knew he was knocked sprawling in the grass.

He tried to pick himself up and scramble out of the way only to be trampled underfoot as more and more pigeons came sailing into the fray. Then almost as suddenly as it began, the tussel was over.

"Break it up you birds!" someone shouted, "Out of the way! Get lost! Scatter I say!" So they all scattered, and in their place stood a giant of a pigeon with his feet planted squarely on the bread.

"Look stranger," he said, glowering fiercely at Homer, "when I say scatter, that goes for you too."

"But-but," stammered Homer, "that's my bread."

"It's my bread now," growled the big one, ruffling up his feathers to make himself look even bigger. "Now whatta ya say to that?"

Before Homer could reply, Sparky the sparrow hopped down beside him. "Take it easy, Homer," he warned. "Forget the bread."

"Like he says," blustered the bully, "better forget it unless you want to get yourself busted up," and he strutted away with the bread in his beak.

"It's not fair," Homer muttered under his breath.

"All's fair at Pigeon Plaza," Sparky explained. "It's every bird for himself. Sometimes it gets rough, so you gotta keep cool."

But Homer was in no mood for advice. For the first time in his life the timid farm pigeon lost his temper. His eyes narrowed to evil slits as he watched the big pigeon perched on the rim of a fountain pecking the raisins out of the bread.

It was too much for Homer, and all at once he exploded. Sailing in feet first, he caught the big one off balance and sent him tumbling into the fountain, KER-SPLOOSH! Then in one whirl and a swoop he snatched up the bread and took off across the park.

Once again there was the mob of greedy pigeons closing in, but this time Homer was ready for them. Before they could head him off he sailed out over the street above the turmoil of traffic and dropped the bread under the wheels of a bus. This infuriated the pigeons. Now they were more determined than ever to catch up with the newcomer.

"Grab his tail feathers!" cried one.

"Peck him on the head!" screamed another. "Give him the works!"

Homer was in such a panic he nearly smacked into a lamppost. At the last second he swerved sharply to the right, then went whirling straight up past the buildings. And with a great roaring of wings the angry mob took up the chase, closing in fast behind him.

They would have caught Homer for sure if he hadn't been so scared. When he was scared Homer could outfly any pigeon. His frenzied wings sent him spiraling up through the curtain of smog at a dizzy pace, high into the sky, well beyond reach of his pursuers. The city pigeons soon realized they were no match for the high-flying farm pigeon.

They were much too out of shape from overeating, and one by
one they dropped out of the chase to go drifting down to the city,
on back to Pigeon Plaza. And Homer had the sky all to himself.

For a few minutes he circled above the city, peering at the jumble of buildings, searching for a quiet place away from the traffic
where he could rest his weary wings.

At the end of a narrow side street Homer discovered a ghostly old building that appeared to be deserted, and as he came down to land on a window ledge there was Sparky the sparrow.

"I saw the whole thing!" he cried gleefully. "That's what I call a fancy bit of flying. Just great! But you sure zonked yourself at Pigeon Plaza. If you ever go back there they'll peck you to a pulp."

"I'm not going back," grumped Homer. "I've had enough of Pigeon Plaza and Mammoth City too. I'm going home."

"But you just got here," said Sparky.

Homer didn't answer. He was wondering about the enormous mechanical arm reaching up toward the building and the huge steel ball swinging back and forth from cables and chains.

"What's that big monster of a thing?" asked the pigeon.

"A wrecking crane. It's a machine that knocks down old buildings," said Sparky.

Then all at once the sparrow realized the steel ball was swinging in their direction and he sprang into the air shouting, "Fly, Homer, fly!" At the same instant there was a resounding BOOM as the steel ball smashed into the building. The wall came tumbling down and Homer took off. But not soon enough. A fragment of flying brick caught him on the wing, and he went careening out of control to disappear in a cloud of dust far below.

After the dust had cleared away Sparky found the pigeon sprawled out in a pile of wreckage. "Zowie!" cried the sparrow, "I thought you were a goner for sure! Are you OK, Homer?"

"I can't tell yet," said the weary pigeon, hauling himself out of the rubble. Then as he waddled out into an alley he found to his dismay that one wing was limp and dragging.

"Looks like you've got a bad flipper," said Sparky. "Can you fly?"

"I'll try," said Homer, and with a good running start he launched himself into the air. But after sailing no more than a few yards the injured wing gave out and he went skidding on his beak.

"Tough luck," sighed the sparrow, "you can't fly home on one motor. And you won't last one night down here. The alley cats or the rats'll get you."

"Then I guess I'm done for," groaned the miserable pigeon.

"Maybe so," said Sparky, "and maybe not. I think I've got an idea," and he hauled a wire coat hanger out of a trash pile, dropping it with a clatter at Homer's feet. "We'll need some extra wing power," he said, "so if you'll just stay put I'll be back in half a jiffy, OK?"

Before Homer could say "OK" the sparrow had darted away
down the alley on around a corner and was gone, leaving the poor
pigeon to wonder what wing power had to do with a coat hanger.
And after what seemed like a very long time Homer began wondering what Sparky meant by "half a jiffy."

It was getting into late afternoon. Deep shadows were closing in everywhere, and the rats were starting to stir about in the trash piles. Still there was no sign of the sparrow and Homer finally decided to give up.

"I'm going home," he muttered, "if I have to walk every step of the way." And he hurried off down the alley in what he guessed to be the right direction. Homer was so intent upon the long perilous journey ahead he didn't see the tomcat crouched in a doorway until it was almost too late.

As the cat sprang out of the doorway the panicky pigeon went fluttering straight up, as high in the air as one wing could carry him, to the top of a stack of packing boxes. There was no place else to go, and he teetered there on the boxes while the cat came climbing up after him.

Just when it seemed that Homer was done for, along came Sparky and a half-dozen friends fluttering up the alley with the coat hanger.

"Hop aboard, Homer! Hop aboard!" Sparky shouted, as they
swooped down for the rescue. And in one desperate leap Homer
was aboard, grabbing onto the coat hanger with both feet. At the
same time the cat's flashing paws caught him on the tail and he lost
a feather. It was that close.

The next thing Homer knew he was sailing past telephone wires up between the buildings with all the sparrows shouting, "It works! It works! Well whatta ya know, it works! What a great invention!"

"It's — it's wonderful," stammered the befuddled pigeon.

"Why don't we call it a sparrowplane?" chortled Sparky.

"Or an airplane hanger," quipped one of the others.

Pretty soon they were gliding along high above the buildings and Sparky was shouting orders to his crew. "Fly straight West into the sun! Full speed ahead!" and with all seven motors whirring at top speed the sparrowplane went zooming across the city through the smog out into the open countryside.

Then once more all the sparrows began to chatter, "Well whatta you know? I can see for miles! What a view! How come! What happened?"

"It's something invisible," cried Sparky, "something called fresh air!" And with perfect visibility and no worries about motor trouble the flight was smooth as could be.

Along toward sunset, the sparrowplane came down for a landing with its motors cut to half speed, gliding over a field then finally on into the barn where the passenger pigeon hopped onto a rafter.

"We've still got a problem," said Sparky. "We can't leave him here all alone. If he can't fly he'll starve."

"Then we'd better stick around," said one sparrow, "at least till the wing gets well."

"Maybe it'll never get well," sighed Homer.

"And maybe it will," said Sparky. "We can always hope."

There was nothing more to be said, and all the sparrows settled themselves on the rafters and were soon sound asleep.

The next day Sparky and his friends were up bright and early chasing about the fields collecting bugs and caterpillars. Feeding Homer turned out to be a fun game, a lively competition to see who could collect the most insects. And they kept the pigeon so well fed there was barely a second between bites.

"If my wing does get well," joked Homer, "I'm afraid I'll be too fat to fly."

Even though he couldn't fly it was a happy time for Homer. With all the sprightly little sparrows flitting in and out, the old barn was now a cheery place, and the days passed quickly.

One morning Homer awakened to find that the stiffness had left the wing. He was ready for a test flight. And he sailed out of the barn up over the fields in an easy glide. Then, with Sparky and all the sparrows cheering him on, he came zooming back to the barn at top speed. The wing was as good as new. Of course Homer was delighted to be flying again, but at the same time it saddened him to think that all his friends would be leaving. Without them it would be lonelier than ever way out there in the country.

"Now that you're all set," chirped Sparky, "I guess we'll be scootin' on back to the city."

"If you don't mind," said one sparrow, "I'd like to stay here."

"Oh, I wish you would," pleaded Homer. "I wish you would."

"If he gets to stay," said another, "then why can't I?"

"What's fair for one is fair for all!" Homer cried joyfully.

"Besides there's plenty of room. You can live here as long as you like."

So they all decided to stay. Sparky and his friends lived there in the old barn just as long as they liked, which turned out to be forever after. And very happily too.